Treasure

belongs to

_____

TIANA
IS MY BABYSITTER

A CENTUM BOOK 978-1-912841-37-0
Published in Great Britain by Centum Books Ltd.
This edition published 2019.

1 3 5 7 9 10 8 6 4 2

Centum Books Ltd, 20 Devon Square, Newton Abbot,
Devon, TQ12 2HR, UK.

www.centumbooksltd.co.uk | books@centumbooksltd.co.uk
CENTUM BOOKS Limited Reg. No. 07641486.

A CIP catalogue record for this book is available
from the British Library.

Printed in China.

DISNEY
PRINCESS

Tiana
Is My Babysitter

By Apple Jordan
Illustrated by Sara Storino and Meritxell Andreu

It was an exciting day for Princess Tiana and Prince Naveen. The prince's family was coming to visit from their homeland, Maldonia.

'Welcome!' Tiana and Naveen said.

Naveen was excited to show his mother, father and little brother, Ralphie, around New Orleans. But Ralphie was tired from travelling such a long distance. He didn't want to go out just yet.

'I can watch Ralphie,' Tiana offered.

'Are you sure you don't mind?' asked Naveen.

'Of course not!' Tiana said. 'It will be fun! I'll invite Lottie and her cousin Max to come over, too.' Ralphie and Max were about the same age. 'I'm sure they have a lot in common.'

'Good idea,' Naveen agreed.

Ralphie and Tiana waved
goodbye to Naveen and the
queen and king as they left for
a day of sightseeing.

When Lottie and Max arrived, Tiana and Lottie
reminisced about all the fun they'd had together when
they were little girls.

They remembered **reading** books in Lottie's bedroom...

... **helping** Tiana's mother in the kitchen...

... and **playing** draughts.

'This will be great!' said Lottie.

'Just like old times,' said Tiana.

But as soon as Tiana introduced the boys to each other, it was clear they had little in common.

'I want to play outside,' said Max.

'I want to stay inside,' said Ralphie, who had already made himself comfortable with a book in a big overstuffed chair.

'Outside!'

'Inside!'

'Uh-oh,' said Tiana. 'This might not be as easy as I thought.'

Tiana came up with a quick solution.
'Let's take turns,' she suggested. 'First we'll play outside.'
Max excitedly ran out the door. Ralphie followed reluctantly.

Max wanted to play badminton, but Ralphie didn't.
Tiana could tell that Ralphie wasn't just being stubborn.
'Have you ever played?' she asked.
Ralphie shook his head shyly. 'And I'm afraid I won't
be any good at it,' he admitted.

'I can teach you,' said Max.

At first Ralphie wasn't good at badminton, but he kept trying. Soon he was hitting the shuttlecock each time Max served it.

'This is fun!' Ralphie said.

When the game ended, it was time to do something inside. Tiana suggested the boys help her and Lottie with a baking project.

'Let's make cupcakes!' Ralphie said.

'Let's make beignets!' said Max.

'Ben-what?' asked Ralphie.

Max explained that a beignet was a pastry and that Tiana made the best beignets in New Orleans.

Ralphie loved cupcakes, but he was tempted by this new dessert.

'Well, I guess I can give it a try,' he said.

Ralphie and Max **mixed** and **measured**.
They **sifted** and **stirred**.

They **rolled** out the **batter**
and **cut it** into **squares**.

After Tiana carefully **fried** each
beignet in hot oil, the boys
sprinkled them with **sugar**.

Ralphie took a bite of a fresh, hot beignet.
'**Mmm,**' he said. '**This is delicious!**'

When snack time was over, Tiana and Lottie took the boys
to Tiana's Palace to hear Louis's band practice.

'A-one, and a-two, and a-one, two, three,' Louis said, conducting.
Then he joined in and blew his trumpet to the beat. 'Why don't the
boys play, too?' he suggested when the band had finished the song.

Ralphie and Max each chose an instrument.

Ralphie banged on the drums. **Boom! Boom! Boom!**
Max blew into a horn. **TOOT!**

But Ralphie's drums were so loud, Max couldn't hear himself play. And Max's horn hurt Ralphie's ears.

'This is no fun,' said Ralphie.

'No fun at all,' said Max.

Finally, they agreed on something!

Tiana suggested the boys take turns.

'Listen to each other play,' she said,
'and then try to join in.'

Max went first, blowing sweetly into his horn.
Root-a-toot-toot.

Then it was Ralphie's turn. He drummed lightly.
Rat-a-tat-tat.

Soon Tiana and Lottie joined
the band, too.

Ralphie and Max might have got off to a rough start, but by the end of the day, they had become good friends.

'I don't remember us having such a hard time getting along when we were young,' Lottie said to Tiana.

'Me neither,' said Tiana. But then they both thought a bit more.

'Well, maybe we didn't agree on everything...,' said Tiana.

'But we always found a way to work things out,'
said Lottie.

'We sure did,' said Tiana. 'Just like Ralphie
and Max!'

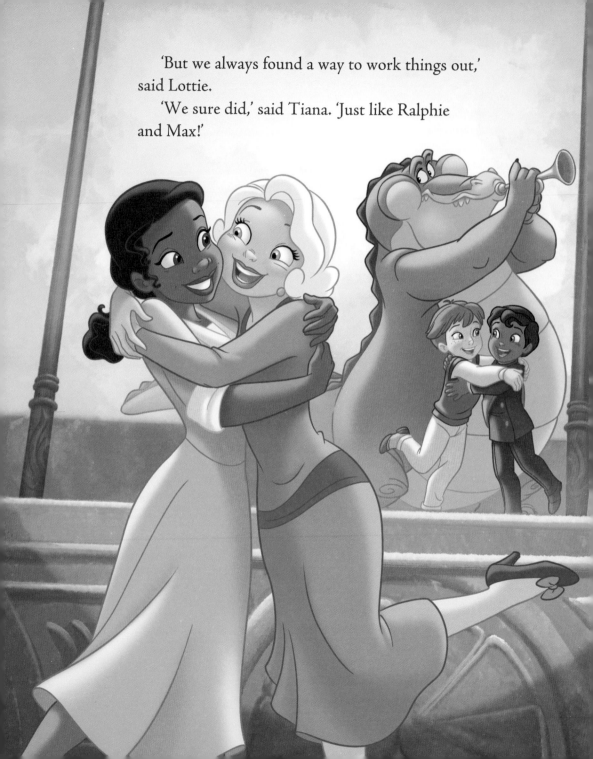

Treasure Cove Stories

Book list may be subject to change.